MADAME DE TREYMES

EDITH
WHARTON

MADAME DE TREYMES

penguin books

PENGUIN BOOKS

Published by the Penguin Group

Penguin Books USA Inc., 375 Hudson Street,
New York, New York 10014, U.S.A.
Penguin Books Ltd, 27 Wrights Lane, London W8 5TZ, England
Penguin Books Australia Ltd, Ringwood, Victoria, Australia
Penguin Books Canada Ltd, 10 Alcorn Avenue,
Toronto, Ontario, Canada M4V 3B2
Penguin Books (N.Z.) Ltd, 182–190 Wairau Road,
Auckland 10, New Zealand

Penguin Books Ltd, Registered Offices:
Harmondsworth, Middlesex, England

First published in 1907
Published in Penguin Books 1995

ISBN 0 14 60.0015 3

Printed in the United States of America

I

John Durham, while he waited for Madame de Malrive to draw on her gloves, stood in the hotel doorway looking out across the Rue de Rivoli at the afternoon brightness of the Tuileries gardens.

His European visits were infrequent enough to have kept unimpaired the freshness of his eye, and he was always struck anew by the vast and consummately ordered spectacle of Paris: by its look of having been boldly and deliberately planned as a background for the enjoyment of life, instead of being forced into grudging concessions to the festive instincts, or barricading itself against them in unenlightened ugliness, like his own lamentable New York.

But today, if the scene had never presented itself more alluringly, in that moist spring bloom between showers, when the horse-chestnuts dome themselves in unreal green against a gauzy sky, and the very dust of the pavement seems the fragrance of lilac made visible – today for the first time the sense of a personal stake in it all, of having to reckon individually with its effects and influences, kept Durham from an unrestrained yielding to the spell. Paris might still be – to the unimplicated it doubtless still was –

the most beautiful city in the world; but whether it were the most lovable or the most detestable depended for him, in the last analysis, on the buttoning of the white glove over which Fanny de Malrive still lingered.

The mere fact of her having forgotten to draw on her gloves as they were descending in the hotel lift from his mother's drawing-room was, in this connection, charged with significance to Durham. She was the kind of woman who always presents herself to the mind's eye as completely equipped, as made up of exquisitely cared for and finely related details; and that the heat of her parting with his family should have left her unconscious that she was emerging gloveless into Paris, seemed, on the whole, to speak hopefully for Durham's future opinion of the city.

Even now, he could detect a certain confusion, a desire to draw breath and catch up with life, in the way she dawdled over the last buttons in the dimness of the porte-cochère, while her footman, outside, hung on her retarded signal.

When at length they emerged, it was to learn from that functionary that Madame la Marquise's carriage had been obliged to yield its place at the door, but was at the moment in the act of regaining it. Madame de Malrive cut the explanation short. 'I shall walk home. The carriage this evening at eight.'

As the footman turned away, she raised her eyes for the first time to Durham's.

'Will you walk with me? Let us cross the Tuileries. I should like to sit a moment on the terrace.'

She spoke quite easily and naturally, as if it were the most commonplace thing in the world for them to be straying afoot together over Paris; but even his vague knowledge of the world she lived in – a knowledge mainly acquired through the perusal of yellow-backed fiction – gave a thrilling significance to her naturalness. Durham, indeed, was beginning to find that one of the charms of a sophisticated society is that it lends point and perspective to the slightest contact between the sexes. If, in the old unrestricted New York days, Fanny Frisbee, from a brown-stone doorstep, had proposed that they should take a walk in the Park, the idea would have presented itself to her companion as agreeable but unimportant; whereas Fanny de Malrive's suggestion that they should stroll across the Tuileries was obviously fraught with unspecified possibilities.

He was so throbbing with the sense of these possibilities that he walked beside her without speaking down the length of the wide alley which follows the line of the Rue de Rivoli, suffering her even, when they reached its farthest end, to direct him in silence up the steps to the terrace of the Feuillants. For, after all, the possibilities were double-faced, and her bold departure from custom might simply mean that what she had to say was so dreadful that it needed all the tenderest mitigation of circumstance.

There was apparently nothing embarrassing to her in his silence: it was a part of her long European discipline that she had learned to manage pauses with ease. In her Frisbee days she might have packed this one with a random fluency; now she was content to let it widen slowly before them like the spacious prospect opening at their feet. The complicated beauty of this prospect, as they moved toward it between the symmetrically clipped limes of the lateral terrace, touched him anew through her nearness, as with the hint of some vast impersonal power, controlling and regulating her life in ways he could not guess, putting between himself and her the whole width of the civilization into which her marriage had absorbed her. And there was such fear in the thought – he read such derision of what he had to offer in the splendour of the great avenues tapering upward to the sunset glories of the Arch – that all he had meant to say when he finally spoke compressed itself at last into an abrupt unmitigated: 'Well?'

She answered at once – as though she had only awaited the call of the national interrogation – 'I don't know when I have been so happy.'

'So happy?' The suddenness of his joy flushed up through his fair skin.

'As I was just now – taking tea with your mother and sisters.'

Durham's 'Oh!' of surprise betrayed also a note of

disillusionment, which she met only by the reconciling murmur: 'Shall we sit down?'

He found two of the springy yellow chairs indigenous to the spot, and placed them under the tree near which they had paused, saying reluctantly, as he did so: 'Of course it was an immense pleasure to *them* to see you again.'

'Oh, not in the same way. I mean –' she paused, sinking into the chair, and betraying, for the first time, a momentary inability to deal becomingly with the situation. 'I mean,' she resumed, smiling, 'that it was not an event for them, as it was for me.'

'An event?' he caught her up again, eagerly; for what, in the language of any civilization, could that word mean but just the one thing he most wished it to?

'To be with dear, good, sweet, simple, real Americans again!' she burst out, heaping up her epithets with reckless prodigality.

Durham's smile once more faded to impersonality, as he rejoined, just a shade on the defensive: 'If it's merely our Americanism you enjoyed – I've no doubt we can give you all you want in that line.'

'Yes, it's just that! But if you knew what the word means to me! It means – it means –' she paused as if to assure herself that they were sufficiently isolated from the desultory groups beneath the other trees – 'it means that I'm *safe* with them; as safe as in a bank!'

Durham felt a sudden warmth behind his eyes and in his throat. 'I think I do know —'

'No, you don't, really; you can't know how dear and strange and familiar it all sounded: the old New York names that kept coming up in your mother's talk, and her charming quaint ideas about Europe — they're all regarding it as a great big innocent pleasure-ground and shop for Americans; and your mother's missing the home-made bread and preferring the American asparagus — I'm so tired of Americans who despise even their own asparagus! And then your married sister's spending her summers at — where is it? — the Kittawittany House on Lake Pohunk —'

A vision of earnest women in Shetland shawls, with spectacles and thin knobs of hair, eating blueberry pie at unwholesome hours in a shingled dining-room on a bare New England hill-top, rose pallidly between Durham and the verdant brightness of the Champs Elysées, and he protested with a slight smile: 'Oh, but my married sister is the black sheep of the family — the rest of us never sank as low as that.'

'Low? I think it's beautiful — fresh and innocent and simple. I remember going to such a place once. They have early dinner — rather late — and go off in buckboards over terrible roads, and bring back golden rod and autumn leaves, and read nature books aloud on the piazza; and there is always one shy young man in flannels — only one — who has come to see the prettiest girl (though how he can choose among so many!) and who takes her off in a buggy for hours and hours –' She paused and summed up with a long sigh: 'It is fifteen years since I was in America.'

'And you're still so good an American.'

'Oh, a better and better one every day!'

He hesitated. 'Then why did you never come back?'

Her face altered instantly, exchanging its retrospective light for the look of slightly shadowed watchfulness which he had known as most habitual to it.

'It was impossible – it has always been so. My husband would not go; and since – since our separation – there have been family reasons.'

Durham sighed impatiently. 'Why do you talk of reasons? The truth is, you have made your life here. You could never give all this up!' He made a discouraged gesture in the direction of the Place de la Concorde.

'Give it up! I would go tomorrow! But it could never, now, be for more than a visit. I must live in France on account of my boy.'

Durham's heart gave a quick beat. At last the talk had neared the point toward which his whole mind was straining, and he began to feel a personal application in her words. But that made him all the more cautious about choosing his own.

'It is an agreement – about the boy?' he ventured.

'I gave my word. They knew that was enough,' she said 7

proudly; adding, as if to put him in full possession of her reasons: 'It would have been much more difficult for me to obtain complete control of my son if it had not been understood that I was to live in France.'

'That seems fair,' Durham assented after a moment's reflection: it was his instinct, even in the heat of personal endeavour, to pause a moment on the question of 'fairness'. The personal claim reasserted itself as he added tentatively: 'But when he *is* brought up — when he's grown up: then you would feel freer?'

She received this with a start, as a possibility too remote to have entered into her view of the future. 'He is only eight years old!' she objected.

'Ah, of course it would be a long way off?'

'A long way off; thank heaven! French mothers part late with their sons, and in that one respect I mean to be a French mother.'

'Of course — naturally — since he has only you,' Durham again assented.

He was eager to show how fully he took her point of view, if only to dispose her to the reciprocal fairness of taking his when the time came to present it. And he began to think that the time had now come; that their walk would not have thus resolved itself, without excuse or pretext, into a tranquil session beneath the trees, for any purpose less important than that of giving him his opportunity.

8 He took it, characteristically, without seeking a trans-

ition. 'When I spoke to you, the other day, about myself – about what I felt for you – I said nothing of the future, because, for the moment, my mind refused to travel beyond its immediate hope of happiness. But I felt, of course, even then, that the hope involved various difficulties – that we can't, as we might once have done, come together without any thought but for ourselves; and whatever your answer is to be, I want to tell you now that I am ready to accept my share of the difficulties.' He paused, and then added explicitly, 'If there's the least chance of your listening to me, I'm willing to live over here as long as you can keep your boy with you.'

II

Whatever Madame de Malrive's answer was to be, there could be no doubt as to her readiness to listen. She received Durham's words without sign of resistance, and took time to ponder them gently before she answered, in a voice touched by emotion, 'You are very generous – very unselfish; but when you fix a limit – no matter how remote – to my remaining here, I see how wrong it is to let myself consider for a moment such possibilities as we have been talking of.'

'Wrong? Why should it be wrong?'

'Because I shall want to keep my boy always! Not, of course, in the sense of living with him, or even forming an important part of his life; I am not deluded enough to think that possible. But I do believe it possible never to pass wholly out of his life; and while there is a hope of that, how can I leave him?' She paused, and turned on him a new face, a face on which the past of which he was still so ignorant showed itself like a shadow suddenly darkening a clear pane. 'How can I make you understand?' she went on urgently. 'It is not only because of my love for him – not only, I mean, because of my own happiness in being with him; that I can't, in imagination, surrender even the remotest hour of his future; it is because, the moment he passes out of my influence, he passes under that other — the influence I have been fighting against every hour since he was born! — I don't mean, you know,' she added, as Durham, with bent head, continued to offer her the silent fixity of his attention, 'I don't mean the special personal influence — except inasmuch as it represents something wider, more general, something that encloses and circulates through the whole world in which he belongs. That is what I meant when I said you could never understand! There is nothing in your experience — in any American experience — to correspond with that far-reaching family organization, which is itself a part of the larger system, and which encloses a young man of my son's position in a network of accepted prejudices and opinions. Everything is prepared in advance — his political and religious convictions, his judgments of people, his sense of honour, his ideas of women, his whole view of life. He is taught to see vileness and corruption in every one not of his own way of thinking, and in every idea that does not directly serve the religious and political purposes of his class. The truth isn't a fixed thing: it's not used to test actions by, it's tested by them, and made to fit in with them. And this forming of the mind begins with the child's first consciousness; it's in his nursery stories, his baby prayers, his very games with his playmates! Already he is only half mine, because the Church has the other half, and will be reaching out for my share as soon as his education begins. But that other half is still mine, and I mean to make it the strongest and most living half of the two, so that, when the inevitable conflict begins, the energy and the truth and the endurance shall be on my side and not on theirs!'

She paused, flushing with the repressed fervour of her utterance, though her voice had not been raised beyond its usual discreet modulations; and Durham felt himself tingling with the transmitted force of her resolve. Whatever shock her words brought to his personal hope, he was grateful to her for speaking them so clearly, for having so sure a grasp of her purpose.

Her decision strengthened his own, and after a pause of deliberation he said quietly: 'There might be a good deal to urge on the other side – the ineffectualness of your sacrifice, the probability that when your son marries he will inevitably be absorbed back into the life of his class and his people; but I can't look at it in that way, because if I were in your place I believe I should feel just as you do about it. As long as there was a fighting chance I should want to keep hold of my half, no matter how much the struggle cost me. And one reason why I understand your feeling about your boy is that I have the same feeling about *you*: as long as there's a fighting chance of keeping my half of you – the half he is willing to spare me – I don't see how I can ever give it up.' He waited again, and then brought out firmly: 'If you'll marry me, I'll agree to live out here as long as you want, and we'll be two instead of one to keep hold of your half of him.'

He raised his eyes as he ended, and saw that hers met them through a quick clouding of tears.

'Ah, I am glad to have had this said to me! But I could never accept such an offer.'

He caught instantly at the distinction. 'That doesn't mean that you could never accept *me*?'

'Under such conditions –'

'But if I am satisfied with the conditions? Don't think that I am speaking rashly, under the influence of the moment. I have expected something of this sort, and I have thought out my side of the case. As far as material circumstances go, I have worked long enough and successfully enough to take my ease and take it where I choose. I mention that because the life I offer you is offered to your boy as well.' He let this sink into her mind before summing up gravely: 'The offer I make is made deliberately, and at least I have a right to a direct answer.'

She was silent again, and then lifted a cleared gaze to his. 'My direct answer then is: if I were still Fanny Frisbee I would marry you.'

He bent toward her persuasively. 'But you will be – when the divorce is pronounced.'

'Ah, the divorce –' She flushed deeply, with an   13

instinctive shrinking back of her whole person which made him straighten himself in his chair.

'Do you so dislike the idea?'

'The idea of divorce? No – not in my case. I should like anything that would do away with the past – obliterate it all – make everything new in my life!'

'Then what – ?' he began again, waiting with the patience of a wooer on the uneasy circling of her tormented mind.

'Oh, don't ask me; I don't know; I am frightened.'

Durham gave a deep sigh of discouragement. 'I thought your coming here with me today – and above all your going with me just now to see my mother – was a sign that you were *not* frightened!'

'Well, I was not when I was with your mother. She made everything seem easy and natural. She took me back into that clear American air where there are no obscurities, no mysteries –'

'What obscurities, what mysteries, are you afraid of?'

She looked about her with a faint shiver. 'I am afraid of everything!' she said.

'That's because you are alone; because you've no one to turn to. I'll clear the air for you fast enough if you'll let me.'

He looked forth defiantly, as if flinging his challenge at the great city which had come to typify the powers contending with him for her possession.

'You say that so easily! But you don't know; none of you know.'

'Know what?'

'The difficulties –'

'I told you I was ready to take my share of the difficulties – and my share naturally includes yours. You know Americans are great hands at getting over difficulties.' He drew himself up confidently. 'Just leave that to me – only tell me exactly what you're afraid of.'

She paused again, and then said: 'The divorce, to begin with – they will never consent to it.'

He noticed that she spoke as though the interests of the whole clan, rather than her husband's individual claim, were to be considered; and the use of the plural pronoun shocked his free individualism like a glimpse of some dark feudal survival.

'But you are absolutely certain of your divorce! I've consulted – of course without mentioning names –'

She interrupted him, with a melancholy smile: 'Ah, so have I. The divorce would be easy enough to get, if they ever let it come into the courts.'

'How on earth can they prevent that?'

'I don't know; my never knowing how they will do things is one of the secrets of their power.'

'Their power? What power?' he broke in with irrepressible contempt. 'Who are these bogeys whose machinations are going to arrest the course of justice in a – comparatively 15

– civilized country? You've told me yourself that Monsieur de Malrive is the least likely to give you trouble; and the others are his uncle the Abbé, his mother and sister. That kind of a syndicate doesn't scare me much. A priest and two women *contra mundum*!'

She shook her head. 'Not *contra mundum*, but with it, their whole world is behind them. It's that mysterious solidarity that you can't understand. One doesn't know how far they may reach, or in how many directions. I have never known. They have always cropped up where I least expected them.'

Before this persistency of negation Durham's buoyancy began to flag, but his determination grew the more fixed.

'Well, then, supposing them to possess these supernatural powers; do you think it's to people of that kind that I'll ever consent to give you up?'

She raised a half-smiling glance of protest. 'Oh, they're not wantonly wicked. They'll leave me alone as long as –'

'As I do?' he interrupted. 'Do you want me to leave you alone? Was that what you brought me here to tell me?'

The directness of the challenge seemed to gather up the scattered strands of her hesitation, and lifting her head she turned on him a look in which, but for its underlying shadow, he might have recovered the full free beam of Fanny Frisbee's gaze.

'I don't know why I brought you here,' she said gently,

'except from the wish to prolong a little the illusion of

being once more an American among Americans. Just now, sitting there with your mother and Katy and Nannie, the difficulties seemed to vanish; the problems grew as trivial to me as they are to you. And I wanted them to remain so a little longer; I wanted to put off going back to them. But it was of no use – they were waiting for me here. They are over there now in that house across the river. She indicated the grey sky-line of the Faubourg, shining in the splintered radiance of the sunset beyond the long sweep of the quays. 'They are a part of me – I belong to them. I must go back to them!' she sighed.

She rose slowly to her feet, as though her metaphor had expressed an actual fact and she felt herself bodily drawn from his side by the influences of which she spoke.

Durham had risen too. 'Then I go back with you!' he exclaimed energetically; and as she paused, wavering a little under the shock of his resolve: 'I don't mean into your house – but into your life!' he said.

She suffered him, at any rate, to accompany her to the door of the house, and allowed their debate to prolong itself through the almost monastic quiet of the quarter which led thither. On the way, he succeeded in wresting from her the confession that, if it were possible to ascertain in advance that her husband's family would not oppose her action, she might decide to apply for a divorce. Short of a positive assurance on this point, she made it clear that she would never move in the matter; there must be no scandal, no *retentissement*, nothing which her boy, necessarily brought up in the French tradition of scrupulously preserved appearances, could afterward regard as the faintest blur on his much-quartered escutcheon. But even this partial concession again raised fresh obstacles; for there seemed to be no one to whom she could entrust so delicate an investigation, and to apply directly to the Marquis de Malrive or his relatives appeared, in the light of her past experience, the last way of learning their intentions.

'But,' Durham objected, beginning to suspect a morbid fixity of idea in her perpetual attitude of distrust – 'but surely you have told me that your husband's sister – what is her name? Madame de Treymes? – was the most powerful member of the group, and that she has always been on your side.'

She hesitated. 'Yes, Christiane has been on my side. She dislikes her brother. But it would not do to ask her.'

'But could no one else ask her? Who are her friends?'

'She has a great many, and some, of course, are mine. But in a case like this they would be all hers; they wouldn't hesitate a moment between us.'

'Why should it be necessary to hesitate between you? Suppose Madame de Treymes sees the reasonableness of what you ask; suppose, at any rate, she sees the hopelessness of opposing you? Why should she make a mystery of your opinion?'

'It's not that; it is that, if I went to her friends, I should never get her real opinion from them. At least I should never know if it *was* her real opinion; and therefore I should be no farther advanced. Don't you see?'

Durham struggled between the sentimental impulse to soothe her, and the practical instinct that it was a moment for unmitigated frankness.

'I'm not sure that I do; but if you can't find out what Madame de Treymes thinks, I'll see what I can do myself.'

'Oh – *you*!' broke from her in mingled terror and admiration; and pausing on her doorstep to lay her hand in his before she touched the bell, she added with a half-whimsical flash of regret: 'Why didn't this happen to Fanny Frisbee?'

III

Why had it not happened to Fanny Frisbee?

Durham put the question to himself as he walked back along the quays, in a state of inner commotion which left him, for once, insensible to the ordered beauty of his surroundings. Propinquity had not been lacking: he had known Miss Frisbee since his college days. In unsophisticated circles, one family is apt to quote another; and the Durham ladies had always quoted the Frisbees. The Frisbees were bold, experienced, enterprising: they had what the novelists of the day called 'dash'. The beautiful Fanny was especially dashing; she had the showiest national attributes, tempered only by a native grace of softness, as the beam of her eyes was subdued by the length of their lashes. And yet young Durham, though not unsusceptible to such charms, had remained content to enjoy them from a safe distance of good fellowship. If he had been asked why, he could not have told; but the Durham of forty understood. It was because there were, with minor modifications, many other Fanny Frisbees; whereas never before, within his ken, had there been a Fanny de Malrive.

He had felt it in a flash, when, the autumn before, he had run across her one evening in the dining-room of the

Beaurivage at Ouchy; when, after a furtive exchange of glances, they had simultaneously arrived at recognition, followed by an eager pressure of hands, and a long evening of reminiscence on the starlit terrace. She was the same, but so mysteriously changed! And it was the mystery, the sense of unprobed depths of initiation, which drew him to her as her freshness had never drawn him. He had not hitherto attempted to define the nature of the change: it remained for his sister Nannie to do that when, on his return to the Rue de Rivoli, where the family were still sitting in conclave upon their recent visitor, Miss Durham summed up their groping comments in the phrase: 'I never saw anything so French!'

Durham, understanding what his sister's use of the epithet implied, recognized it instantly as the explanation of his own feelings. Yes, it was the finish, the modelling which Madame de Malrive's experience had given her that set her apart from the fresh uncomplicated personalities of which she had once been simply the most charming type. The influences that had lowered her voice, regulated her gestures, toned her down to harmony with the warm dim background of a long social past – these influences had lent to her natural fineness of perception a command of expression adapted to complex conditions. She had moved in surroundings through which one could hardly bounce and bang on the genial American plan without knocking the angles off a number of sacred institutions;

and her acquired dexterity of movement seemed to Durham a crowning grace. It was a shock, now that he knew at what cost the dexterity had been acquired, to acknowledge this even to himself; he hated to think that she could owe anything to such conditions as she had been placed in. And it gave him a sense of the tremendous strength of the organisation into which she had been absorbed, that in spite of her horror, her moral revolt, she had not reacted against its external forms. She might abhor her husband, her marriage, and the world to which it had introduced her, but she had become a product of that world in its outward expression, and no better proof of the fact was needed than her exotic enjoyment of Americanism.

The sense of the distance to which her American past had been removed was never more present to him than when, a day or two later, he went with his mother and sister to return her visit. The region beyond the river existed, for the Durham ladies, only as the unmapped environment of the Bon Marché; and Nannie Durham's exclamation on the pokiness of the streets and the dullness of the houses showed Durham, with a start, how far he had already travelled from the family point of view.

'Well, if this is all she got by marrying a Marquis!' the young lady summed up as they paused before the small sober hotel in its high-walled court; and Katy, following

her mother through the stone-vaulted and stone-floored

vestibule, murmured: 'It must be simply freezing in winter.'

In the softly-faded drawing-room, with its old pastels in old frames, its windows looking on the damp green twilight of a garden sunk deep in blackened walls, the American ladies might have been even more conscious of the insufficiency of their friend's compensations, had not the warmth of her welcome precluded all other reflections. It was not till she had gathered them about her in the corner beside the tea-table, that Durham identified the slender dark lady loitering negligently in the background, and introduced in a comprehensive murmur to the American group, as the redoubtable sister-in-law to whom he had declared himself ready to throw down his challenge.

There was nothing very redoubtable about Madame de Treymes, except perhaps the kindly yet critical observation which she bestowed on her sister-in-law's visitors: the unblinking attention of a civilized spectator observing an encampment of aborigines. He had heard of her as a beauty, and was surprised to find her, as Nannie afterward put it, a mere stick to hang clothes on (but they *did* hang!), with a small brown glancing face, like that of a charming little inquisitive animal. Yet before she had addressed ten words to him – nibbling at the hard English consonants like nuts – he owned the justice of the epithet. She was a beauty, if beauty, instead of being restricted to the cast of the face, is a pervasive attribute informing the hands, the voice, the gestures, the very fall of a flounce and tilt of a feather. In this impalpable *aura* of grace Madame de Treymes' dark meagre presence unmistakably moved, like a thin flame in a wide quiver of light. And as he realized that she looked much handsomer than she was, so, while they talked, he felt that she understood a great deal more than she betrayed. It was not through the groping speech which formed their apparent medium of communication that she imbibed her information: she found it in the air, she extracted it from Durham's look and manner, she caught it in the turn of her sister-in-law's defenceless eyes – for in her presence Madame de Malrive became Fanny Frisbee again! – she put it together, in short, out of just such unconsidered, indescribable trifles as differentiated the quiet felicity of her dress from Nannie and Katy's 'handsome' haphazard clothes.

Her actual converse with Durham moved, meanwhile, strictly in the conventional ruts: had he been long in Paris, which of the new plays did he like best, was it true that American *jeunes filles* were sometimes taken to the Boulevard theatres? And she threw an interrogative glance at the young ladies beside the tea-table. To Durham's reply that it depended how much French they knew, she shrugged and smiled, replying that his compatriots all spoke French like Parisians, inquiring, after a moment's thought, if they learned it, *là-bas, des nègres,* and laughing heartily when Durham's astonishment revealed her blunder.

When at length she had taken leave – enveloping the Durham ladies in a last puzzled, penetrating look – Madame de Malrive turned to Mrs Durham with a faintly embarrassed smile.

'My sister-in-law was much interested: I believe you are the first Americans she has ever known.'

'Good gracious!' ejaculated Nannie, as though such social darkness required immediate missionary action on someone's part.

'Well, she knows *us*,' said Durham, catching, in Madame de Malrive's rapid glance, a startled assent to his point.

'After all,' reflected the accurate Katy, as though seeking an excuse for Madame de Treymes' unenlightenment, '*we* don't know many French people, either.'

To which Nannie promptly if obscurely retorted: 'Ah, but we couldn't and *she* could!'

IV

Madame de Treymes' friendly observation of her sister-in-law's visitors resulted in no expression on her part of a desire to renew her study of them. To all appearances, she passed out of their lives when Madame de Malrive's door closed on her; and Durham felt that the arduous task of making her acquaintance was still to be begun.

He felt also, more than ever, the necessity of attempting it; and in his determination to lose no time, and his perplexity how to set most speedily about the business, he bethought himself of applying to his cousin Mrs Boykin.

Mrs Elmer Boykin was a small plump woman, to whose vague prettiness the lines of middle-age had given no meaning: as though whatever had happened to her had merely added to the sum total of her inexperience. After a Parisian residence of twenty-five years, spent in a state of feverish servitude to the great artists of the Rue de la Paix, her dress and hair still retained a certain rigidity in keeping with the directness of her gaze and the unmodulated candour of her voice. Her very drawing-room had the hard bright atmosphere of her native skies, and one felt that she was still true at heart to the national ideals in electric lighting and plumbing.

She and her husband had left America owing to the impossibility of living there with the finish and decorum which the Boykin standard demanded; but in the isolation of their exile they had created about them a kind of phantom America, where the national prejudices continued to flourish unchecked by the national progressiveness: a little world sparsely peopled by compatriots in the same attitude of chronic opposition toward a society chronically unaware of them. In this uncontaminated air Mr and Mrs Boykin had preserved the purity of simpler conditions, and Elmer Boykin, returning rakishly from a Sunday's racing at Chantilly, betrayed, under his 'knowing' coat and the racing-glasses slung ostentatiously across his shoulder, the unmistakable cut of the American business man coming 'up town' after a long day in the office.

It was a part of the Boykins' uncomfortable but determined attitude – and perhaps a last expression of their latent patriotism – to live in active disapproval of the world about them, fixing in memory with little stabs of reprobation innumerable instances of what the abominable foreigner was doing; so that they reminded Durham of persons peacefully following the course of a horrible war by pricking red pins in a map. To Mrs Durham, with her gentle tourist's view of the European continent, as a vast Museum in which the human multitudes simply furnished the element of costume, the Boykins seemed abysmally instructed, and darkly expert in forbidden things; and her son, without sharing her simple faith in their omniscience, credited them with an ample supply of the kind of information of which he was in search.

Mrs Boykin, from the corner of an intensely modern Gobelin sofa, studied her cousin as he balanced himself insecurely on one of the small gilt chairs which always look surprised at being sat in.

'Fanny de Malrive? Oh, of course: I remember you were all very intimate with the Frisbees when they lived in West Thirty-third Street. But she has dropped all her American friends since her marriage. The excuse was that de Malrive didn't like them but as she's been separated for five or six years, I can't see – You say she's been very nice to your mother and the girls? Well, I daresay she is beginning to feel the need of friends she can really trust; for as for her French relations – ! That Malrive set is the worst in the Faubourg. Of course you know what *he* is; even the family, for decency's sake, had to back her up, and urge her to get a separation. And Christiane de Treymes –'

Durham seized his opportunity. 'Is she so very reprehensible too?'

Mrs Boykin pursed up her small colourless mouth. 'I can't speak from personal experience. I know Madame de Treymes slightly – I have met her at Fanny's – but she never remembers the fact except when she wants me to go to one of her *ventes de charité*. They all remember us then; and some American women are silly enough to ruin themselves at the smart bazaars, and fancy they will get invitations in return. They say Mrs Addison G. Pack followed Madame d'Alglade around for a whole winter, and spent a hundred thousand francs at her stalls; and at the end of the season Madame d'Alglade asked her to tea, and when she got there she found *that* was for a charity too, and she had to pay a hundred francs to get in.'

Mrs Boykin paused with a smile of compassion. 'That is not *my* way,' she continued. 'Personally I have no desire to thrust myself into French society – I can't see how any American woman can do so without loss of self-respect. But any one can tell you about Madame de Treymes.'

'I wish you would, then,' Durham suggested.

'Well, I think Elmer had better,' said his wife mysteriously, as Mr Boykin, at this point, advanced across the wide expanse of Aubusson on which his wife and Durham were islanded in a state of propinquity without privacy.

'What's that, Bessy? Hah, Durham, how are you? Didn't see you at Auteuil this afternoon. You don't race? Busy sight-seeing, I suppose? What was that my wife was telling you? Oh, about Madame de Treymes.'

He stroked his pepper-and-salt moustache with a gesture intended rather to indicate than to conceal the smile of experience beneath it. 'Well, Madame de Treymes has not been like a happy country – she's had a history: several of 'em. Someone said she constituted the *feuilleton* of the Faubourg daily news. *La suite au prochain numéro –* you see the point? Not that I speak from personal knowledge. Bessy and I have never cared to force our way –' He paused, reflecting that his wife had probably anticipated him in the expression of this familiar sentiment, and added with a significant nod: 'Of course you know the Prince d'Armillac by sight? No? I'm surprised at that. Well, he's one of the choicest ornaments of the Jockey Club: very fascinating to the ladies I believe, but the deuce and all at baccarat. Ruined his mother and a couple of maiden aunts already – and now Madame de Treymes has put the family pearls up the spout, and is wearing imitation for love of him.'

'I had that straight from my maid's cousin, who is employed by Madame d'Armillac's jeweller,' said Mrs Boykin with conscious pride.

'Oh, it's straight enough – more than *she* is!' retorted her husband, who was slightly jealous of having his facts reinforced by any information not of his own gleaning.

'Be careful of what you say, Elmer,' Mrs Boykin interposed with archness. 'I suspect John of being seriously smitten by the lady.'

Durham let this pass unchallenged, submitting with a good grace to his host's low whistle of amusement, and the sardonic inquiry: 'Ever do anything with the foils? D'Armillac is what they call over here a *fine lame*.'

'Oh, I don't mean to resort to bloodshed unless it's

absolutely necessary; but I mean to make the lady's acquaintance,' said Durham, falling into his key.

Mrs Boykin's lips tightened to the vanishing point. 'I am afraid you must apply for an introduction to more fashionable people than *we* are. Elmer and I so thoroughly disapprove of French society that we have always declined to take any part in it. But why should not Fanny de Malrive arrange a meeting for you?'

Durham hesitated. 'I don't think she is on very intimate terms with her husband's family –'

'You mean that she's not allowed to introduce *her* friends to them,' Mrs Boykin interjected sarcastically; while her husband added, with an air of portentous initiation: 'Ah, my dear fellow, the way they treat the Americans over here – that's another chapter, you know.'

'How some people can *stand* it!' Mrs Boykin chimed in; and as the footman, entering at that moment, tendered her a large coroneted envelope, she held it up as if in illustration of the indignities to which her countrymen were subjected.

'Look at that, my dear John,' she exclaimed – 'another card to one of their everlasting bazaars! Why, it's at Madame d'Armillac's, the Prince's mother. Madame de Treymes must have sent it, of course. The brazen way in which they combine religion and immorality! Fifty francs admission – *rien que cela!* – to see some of the most disreputable people in Europe. And if you're an American, you're expected to leave at least a thousand behind you. Their own people naturally get off cheaper.' She tossed over the card to her cousin. 'There's your opportunity to see Madame de Treymes.'

'Make it two thousand, and she'll ask you to tea,' Mr Boykin scathingly added.

V

In the monumental drawing-room of the Hôtel de Malrive – it had been a surprise to the American to read the name of the house emblazoned on black marble over its still more monumental gateway – Durham found himself surrounded by a buzz of feminine tea-sipping oddly out of keeping with the wigged and cuirassed portraits frowning high on the walls, the majestic attitude of the furniture, the rigidity of great gilt consoles drawn up like lords-in-waiting against the tarnished panels.

It was the old Marquise de Malrive's 'day', and Madame de Treymes, who lived with her mother, had admitted Durham to the heart of the enemy's country by inviting him, after his prodigal disbursements at the charity bazaar, to come in to tea on a Thursday. Whether, in thus fulfilling Mr Boykin's prediction, she had been aware of Durham's purpose, and had her own reasons for falling in with it; or whether she simply wished to reward his lavishness at the fair, and permit herself another glimpse of an American so picturesquely embodying the type familiar to French fiction – on these points Durham was still in doubt.

Meanwhile, Madame de Treymes being engaged with a

venerable Duchess in a black shawl – all the older ladies present had the sloping shoulders of a generation of shawl-wearers – her American visitor, left in the isolation of his unimportance, was using it as a shelter for a rapid survey of the scene.

He had begun his study of Fanny de Malrive's situation without any real understanding of her fears. He knew the repugnance to divorce existing in the French Catholic world, but since the French laws sanctioned it, and in a case so flagrant as his injured friend's, would inevitably accord it with the least possible delay and exposure, he could not take seriously any risk of opposition on the part of the husband's family. Madame de Malrive had not become a Catholic, and since her religious scruples could not be played on, the only weapon remaining to the enemy – the threat of fighting the divorce – was one they could not wield without self-injury. Certainly, if the chief object were to avoid scandal, commonsense must counsel Monsieur de Malrive and his friends not to give the courts an opportunity of exploring his past; and since the echo of such explorations, and their ultimate transmission to her son, were what Madame de Malrive most dreaded, the opposing parties seemed to have a common ground for agreement, and Durham could not but regard his friend's fears as the result of over-taxed sensibilities. All this had seemed evident enough to him as he entered the austere portals of the Hôtel de Malrive and passed, between the faded liveries of old family servants, to the presence of the dreaded dowager above. But he had not been ten minutes in that presence before he had arrived at a faint intuition of what poor Fanny meant. It was not in the exquisite mildness of the old Marquise, a little grey-haired bunch of a woman in dowdy mourning, or in the small, neat presence of the priestly uncle, the Abbé, who had so obviously just stepped down from one of the picture-frames overhead: it was not in the aspect of these chief protagonists, so outwardly unformidable, that Durham read an occult danger to his friend. It was rather in their setting, their surroundings, the little company of elderly and dowdy persons – so uniformly clad in weeping blacks and purples that they might have been assembled for some mortuary anniversary – it was in the remoteness and the solidarity of this little group that Durham had his first glimpse of the social force of which Fanny de Malrive had spoken. All these amiably chatting visitors, who mostly bore the stamp of personal insignificance on their mildly sloping or aristocratically beaked faces, hung together in a visible closeness of tradition, dress, attitude, and manner, as different as possible from the loose aggregation of a roomful of his own countrymen. Durham felt, as he observed them, that he had never before known what 'society' meant; nor understood that, in an organized and inherited system, it exists full-fledged where two or three of its members are assembled.

Upon this state of bewilderment, this sense of having entered a room in which the lights had suddenly been turned out, even Madame de Treymes' intensely modern presence threw no illumination. He was conscious, as she smilingly rejoined him, not of her points of difference from the others, but of the myriad invisible threads by which she held to them; he even recognized the audacious slant of her little brown profile in the portrait of a powdered ancestress beneath which she had paused a moment in advancing. She was simply one particular facet of the solid, glittering, impenetrable body which he had thought to turn in his hands and look through like a crystal; and when she said, in her clear staccato English, 'Perhaps you will like to see the other rooms,' he felt like crying out in his blindness: 'If I could only be sure of seeing *anything* here!' Was she conscious of his blindness, and was he as remote and unintelligible to her as she was to him? This possibility, as he followed her through the nobly-unfolding rooms of the great house, gave him his first hope of recoverable advantage. For, after all, he had some vague traditional lights on her world and its ante-cedents; whereas to her he was a wholly new phenomenon, as unexplained as a fragment of meteorite dropped at her feet on the smooth gravel of the garden-path they were pacing.

She had led him down into the garden, in response to his admiring exclamation, and perhaps also because she was sure that, in the chill spring afternoon, they would have its embowered privacies to themselves. The garden was small, but intensely rich and deep – one of those wells of verdure and fragrance which everywhere sweeten the air of Paris by wafts blown above old walls on quiet streets; and as Madame de Treymes paused against the ivy bank masking its farther boundary, Durham felt more than ever removed from the normal bearings of life.

His sense of strangeness was increased by the surprise of his companion's next speech.

'You wish to marry my sister-in-law?' she asked abruptly; and Durham's start of wonder was followed by an immediate feeling of relief. He had expected the preliminaries of their interview to be as complicated as the bargaining in an Eastern bazaar, and had feared to lose himself at the first turn in a labyrinth of 'foreign' intrigue.

'Yes, I do,' he said with equal directness; and they smiled together at the sharp report of question and answer.

The smile put Durham more completely at his ease, and after waiting for her to speak, he added with deliberation: 'So far, however, the wishing is entirely on my side.' His scrupulous conscience felt itself justified in this reserve by the conditional nature of Madame de Malrive's consent.

'I understand; but you have been given reason to hope –'

'Every man in my position gives himself his own reasons for hoping,' he interposed, with a smile.

'I understand that too,' Madame de Treymes assented. 'But still – you spent a great deal of money the other day at our bazaar.'

'Yes: I wanted to have a talk with you, and it was the readiest – if not the most distinguished – means of attracting your attention.'

'I understand,' she once more reiterated, with a gleam of amusement.

'It is because I suspect you of understanding everything that I have been so anxious for this opportunity.'

She bowed her acknowledgment, and said: 'Shall we sit a moment?' adding, as he drew their chairs under a tree, 'You permit me, then, to say that I believe I understand also a little of our good Fanny's mind?'

'On that point I have no authority to speak. I am here only to listen.'

'Listen, then: you have persuaded her that there would be no harm in divorcing my brother – since I believe your religion does not forbid divorce?'

'Madame de Malrive's religion sanctions divorce in such a case as –'

'As my brother has furnished? Yes, I have heard that your race is stricter in judging such *écarts*. But you must not think,' she added, 'that I defend my brother. Fanny must have told you that we have always given her our sympathy.'

'She has let me infer it from her way of speaking of you.'

Madame de Treymes arched her dramatic eyebrows. 'How cautious you are! I am so straightforward that I shall have no chance with you.'

'You will be quite safe, unless you are so straightforward that you put me on my guard.'

She met this with a low note of amusement.

'At this rate we shall never get any farther; and in two minutes I must go back to my mother's visitors. Why should we go on fencing? The situation is really quite simple. Tell me just what you wish to know. I have always been Fanny's friend, and that disposes me to be yours.'

Durham, during this appeal, had had time to steady his thoughts; and the result of his deliberation was that he said, with a return to his former directness: 'Well, then, what I wish to know is, what position your family would take if Madame de Malrive should sue for a divorce?' He added, without giving her time to reply: 'I naturally wish to be clear on this point before urging my cause with your sister-in-law.'

Madame de Treymes seemed in no haste to answer; but after a pause of reflection she said, not unkindly, 'My poor Fanny might have asked me that herself.'

'I beg you to believe that I am not acting as her spokesman," Durham hastily interposed. 'I merely wish to clear up the situation before speaking to her in my own behalf.'

'You are the most delicate of suitors! But I understand your feeling. Fanny also is extremely delicate: it was a great surprise to us at first. Still, in this case –' Madame de Treymes paused – 'since she has no religious scruples, and she had no difficulty in obtaining a separation, why should she fear any in demanding a divorce?'

'I don't know that she does: but the mere fact of possible opposition might be enough to alarm the delicacy you have observed in her.'

'Ah – yes: on her boy's account.'

'Partly, doubtless, on her boy's account.'

'So that, if my brother objects to a divorce, all he has to do is to announce his objection? But, my dear sir, you are giving your case into my hands!' She flashed an amused smile on him.

'Since you say you are Madame de Malrive's friend, could there be a better place for it?'

As she turned her eyes on him he seemed to see, under the flitting lightness of her glance, the sudden concentrated expression of the ancestral will. 'I am Fanny's friend, certainly. But with us family considerations are paramount. And our religion forbids divorce.'

'So that, inevitably, your brother will oppose it?'

She rose from her seat, and stood fretting with her slender boot-tip the minute red pebbles of the path.

'I must really go in; my mother will never forgive me for deserting her.'

'But surely you owe me an answer?' Durham protested, rising also.

'In return for your purchases at my stall?'

'No: in return for the trust I have placed in you.'

She mused on this, moving slowly a step or two towards the house.

'Certainly I wish to see you again; you interest me,' she said smiling. 'But it is so difficult to arrange. If I were to ask you to come here again, my mother and uncle would be surprised. And at Fanny's –'

'Oh, not there!' he exclaimed.

'Where then? Is there any other house where we are likely to meet?'

Durham hesitated; but he was goaded by the flight of the precious minutes. 'Not unless you'll come and dine with me,' he said boldly.

'Dine with you? *Au cabaret?* Ah, that would be diverting – but impossible!'

'Well, dine with my cousin, then – I have a cousin, an American lady, who lives here,' said Durham, with suddenly soaring audacity.

She paused with puzzled brows. 'An American lady whom I know?'

'By name, at any rate. You send her cards for all your charity bazaars.'

She received the thrust with a laugh. 'We do exploit your compatriots.'

'Oh, I don't think she has ever gone to the bazaars.'

'But she might if I dined with her?'

'Still less, I imagine.'

She reflected on this, and then said with acuteness: 'I like that, and I accept – but what is the lady's name?'

VI

On the way home, in the first drop of his exaltation, Durham had said to himself: 'But why on earth should Bessy invite her?'

He had, naturally, 'no very cogent reasons to give Mrs Boykin in support of his astonishing request, and could only, marvelling at his own growth in duplicity, suffer her to infer that he was really, shamelessly 'smitten' with the lady he thus proposed to thrust upon her hospitality. But, to his surprise, Mrs Boykin hardly gave herself time to pause upon his reasons. They were swallowed up in the fact that Madame de Treymes wished to dine with her, as the lesser luminaries vanish in the blaze of the sun.

'I am not surprised,' she declared, with a faint smile intended to check her husband's unruly wonder. 'I wonder *you* are, Elmer. Didn't you tell me that Armillac went out of his way to speak to you the other day at the races? And at Madame d'Alglade's sale – yes, I went there after all, just for a minute, because I found Katy and Nannie were so anxious to be taken – well, that day I noticed that Madame de Treymes was quite *empressée* when we went up to her stall. Oh, I didn't buy anything: I merely waited 43 while the girls chose some lampshades. They thought it would be interesting to take home something painted by a real Marquise, and of course I didn't tell them that those women *never* make the things they sell at their stalls. But I repeat I'm not surprised: I suspected that Madame de Treymes had heard of our little dinners. You know they're really horribly bored in that poky old Faubourg. My poor John, I see now why she's been making up to you! But on one point I am quite determined, Elmer; whatever you say, I shall *not* invite the Prince d'Armillac.'

Elmer, as far as Durham could observe, did not say much; but, like his wife, he continued in a state of pleasantly agitated activity till the momentous evening of the dinner.

The festivity in question was restricted in numbers, either owing to the difficulty of securing suitable guests, or from a desire not to have it appear that Madame de Treymes' hosts attached any special importance to her presence; but the smallness of the company was counterbalanced by the multiplicity of the courses.

The national determination not to be 'downed' by the despised foreigner, to show a wealth of material resource obscurely felt to compensate for the possible lack of other distinctions – this resolve had taken, in Mrs Boykin's case, the shape – or rather the multiple shapes – of a series of culinary feats, of gastronomic combinations, which would have commanded her deep respect had she seen them on any other table, and which she naturally relied on to produce the same effect on her guest. Whether or not the desired result was achieved, Madame de Treymes' manner did not specifically declare; but it showed a general complaisance, a charming willingness to be amused, which made Mr Boykin, for months afterward, allude to her among his compatriots as 'an old friend of my wife's – takes pot-luck with us, you know. Of course there's not a word of truth in any of those ridiculous stories.'

It was only when, to Durham's intense surprise, Mr Boykin hazarded to his neighbour the regret that they had not been so lucky as to 'secure the Prince' – it was then only that the lady showed, not indeed anything so simple and unprepared as embarrassment, but a faint play of wonder, an under-flicker of amusement, as though recognizing that, by some odd law of social compensation, the crudity of the talk might account for the complexity of the dishes.

But Mr Boykin was tremulously alive to hints, and the conversation at once slid to safer topics, easy generalizations which left Madame de Treymes ample time to explore the table, to use her narrowed gaze like a knife slitting open the unsuspicious personalities about her. Nannie and Katy Durham, who, after much discussion (to which their hostess candidly admitted them), had been included in the feast, were the special objects of Madame de Treymes' observation. During dinner she ignored in their favour the other carefully selected guests – the fashionable art-critic, the old Legitimist general, the beauty from the English Embassy, the whole impressive marshalling of Mrs Boykin's social resources – and when the men returned to the drawing-room, Durham found her still fanning in his sisters the flame of an easily kindled enthusiasm. Since she could hardly have been held by the intrinsic interest of their converse, the sight gave him another swift intuition of the working of those hidden forces with which Fanny de Malrive felt herself encompassed. But when Madame de Treymes, at his approach, let him see that it was for him she had been reserving herself, he felt that so graceful an impulse needed no special explanation. She had the art of making it seem quite natural that they should move away together to the remotest of Mrs Boykin's far-drawn salons, and that there, in a glaring privacy of brocade and ormolu, she should turn to him with a smile which avowed her intentional quest of seclusion.

'Confess that I have done a great deal for you!' she exclaimed, making room for him on a sofa judiciously screened from the observation of the other rooms.

'In coming to dine with my cousin?' he inquired, answering her smile.

'Let us say, in giving you this half-hour.'

'For that I am duly grateful – and shall be still more so when I know what it contains for me.'

'Ah, I am not sure. You will not like what I am going to say.'

'Shall I not?' he rejoined, changing colour.

She raised her eyes from the thoughtful contemplation of her painted fan. 'You appear to have no idea of the difficulties.'

'Should I have asked your help if I had not had an idea of them?'

'But you are still confident that with my help you can surmount them?'

'I can't believe you have come here to take that confidence from me?'

She leaned back, smiling at him through her lashes. 'And all this I am to do for your *beaux yeux*?'

'No – for your own: that you may see with them what happiness you are conferring.'

'You are extremely clever, and I like you.' She paused, and then brought out with lingering emphasis: 'But my family will not hear of a divorce.'

She threw into her voice such an accent of finality that Durham, for the moment, felt himself brought up against an insurmountable barrier; but, almost at once, his fear was mitigated by the conviction that she would not have put herself out so much to say so little.

47

'When you speak of your family, do you include yourself?' he suggested.

She threw a surprised glance at him. 'I thought you understood that I am simply their mouthpiece.'

At this he rose quietly to his feet with a gesture of acceptance. 'I have only to thank you, then, for not keeping me longer in suspense.'

His air of wishing to put an immediate end to the conversation seemed to surprise her. 'Sit down a moment longer,' she commanded him kindly; and as he leaned against the back of his chair, without appearing to hear her request, she added in a low voice: 'I am very sorry for you and Fanny – but you are not the only persons to be pitied.'

'The only persons?'

'In our unhappy family.' She touched her breast with a sudden tragic gesture. 'I, for instance, whose help you ask – if you could guess how I need help myself!'

She had dropped her light manner as she might have tossed aside her fan, and he was startled at the intimacy of misery to which her look and movement abruptly admitted him. Perhaps no Anglo-Saxon fully understands the fluency in self-revelation which centuries of the confessional have given to the Latin races, and to Durham, at any rate, Madame de Treymes' sudden avowal gave the shock of a physical abandonment.

'I am so sorry,' he stammered – 'is there any way in
48 which I can be of use to you?'

She sat before him with her hands clasped, her eyes fixed on his in a terrible intensity of appeal. 'If you would – if you would! Oh, there is nothing I would not do for you. I have still a great deal of influence with my mother, and what my mother commands we all do. I could help you – I am sure I could help you; but not if my own situation were known. And if nothing can be done it must be known in a few days.'

Durham had reseated himself at her side. 'Tell me what I can do,' he said in a low tone, forgetting his own preoccupations in his genuine concern for her distress.

She looked up at him through tears. 'How dare I? Your race is so cautious, so self-controlled – you have so little indulgence for the extravagances of the heart. And my folly has been incredible – and unrewarded.' She paused, and as Durham waited in a silence which she guessed to be compassionate, she brought out below her breath: 'I have lent money – my husband's, my brother's – money that was not mine, and now I have nothing to repay it with.'

Durham gazed at her in genuine astonishment. The turn the conversation had taken led quite beyond his uncomplicated experiences with the other sex. She saw his surprise, and extended her hands in deprecation and entreaty. 'Alas, what must you think of me? How can I explain my humiliating myself before a stranger? Only by telling you the whole truth – the fact that I am not alone 49 in this disaster, that I could not confess my situation to my family without ruining myself, and involving in my ruin someone who, however undeservedly, has been as dear to me as – as you are to –'

Durham pushed his chair back with a sharp exclamation.

'Ah, even that does not move you!' she said.

The cry restored him to his senses by the long shaft of light it sent down the dark windings of the situation. He seemed suddenly to know Madame de Treymes as if he had been brought up with her in the inscrutable shades of the Hôtel de Malrive.

She, on her side, appeared to have a startled but uncomprehending sense of the fact that his silence was no longer completely sympathetic, that her touch called forth no answering vibration; and she made a desperate clutch at the one chord she could be certain of sounding.

'You have asked a great deal of me – much more than you can guess. Do you mean to give me nothing – not even your sympathy – in return? Is it because you have heard horrors of me? When are they not said of a woman who is married unhappily? Perhaps not in your fortunate country, where she may seek liberation without dishonour. But here –! You who have seen the consequences of our disastrous marriages – you who may yet be the victim of our cruel and abominable system; have you no pity for one who has suffered in the same way, and without the possibility of release?' She paused, laying her hand on his arm with a smile of deprecating irony. 'It is not because you are not rich. At such times the crudest way is the shortest, and I don't pretend to deny that I know I am asking you a trifle. You Americans, when you want a thing, always pay ten times what it is worth, and I am giving you the wonderful chance to get what you most want at a bargain.'

Durham sat silent, her little gloved hand burning his coat-sleeve as if it had been a hot iron. His brain was tingling with the shock of her confession. She wanted money, a great deal of money: that was clear, but it was not the point. She was ready to sell her influence, and he fancied she could be counted on to fulfil her side of the bargain. The fact that he could so trust her seemed only to make her more terrible to him – more supernaturally dauntless and baleful. For what was it that she exacted of him? She had said she must have money to pay her debts; but he knew that was only a pretext which she scarcely expected him to believe. She wanted the money for someone else; that was what her allusion to a fellow-victim meant. She wanted it to pay the Prince's gambling debts – it was at that price that Durham was to buy the right to marry Fanny de Malrive.

Once the situation had worked itself out in his mind, he found himself unexpectedly relieved of the necessity of weighing the arguments for and against it. All the traditional forces of his blood were in revolt, and he could only surrender himself to their pressure, without thought of compromise or parley.

He stood up in silence, and the abruptness of his movement caused Madame de Treymes' hand to slip from his arm.

'You refuse?' she exclaimed; and he answered with a bow: 'Only because of the return you propose to make me.'

She stood staring at him, in a perplexity so genuine and profound that he could almost have smiled at it through his disgust.

'Ah, you are all incredible,' she murmured at last, stooping to repossess herself of her fan; and as she moved past him to rejoin the group in the farther room, she added in an incisive undertone: 'You are quite at liberty to repeat our conversation to your friend!'

VII

Durham did not take advantage of the permission thus strangely flung at him: of his talk with her sister-in-law he gave to Madame de Malrive only that part which concerned her.

Presenting himself for this purpose, the day after Mrs Boykin's dinner, he found his friend alone with her son; and the sight of the child had the effect of dispelling whatever illusive hopes had attended him to the threshold. Even after the governess's descent upon the scene had left Madame de Malrive and her visitor alone, the little boy's presence seemed to hover admonishingly between them, reducing to a bare statement of fact Durham's confession of the total failure of his errand.

Madame de Malrive heard the confession calmly; she had been too prepared for it not to have prepared a countenance to receive it. Her first comment was: 'I have never known them to declare themselves so plainly –' and Durham's baffled hopes fastened themselves eagerly on the words. Had she not always warned him that there was nothing so misleading as their plainness? And might it not be that, in spite of his advisedness, he had suffered too easy a rebuff? But second thoughts reminded him that the 53 refusal had not been as unconditional as his necessary reservations made it seem in the repetition; and that, furthermore, it was his own act, and not that of his opponents, which had determined it. The impossibility of revealing this to Madame de Malrive only made the difficulty shut in more darkly around him, and in the completeness of his discouragement he scarcely needed her reminder of his promise to regard the subject as closed when once the other side had defined its position.

He was secretly confirmed in this acceptance of his fate by the knowledge that it was really he who had defined the position. Even now that he was alone with Madame de Malrive, and subtly aware of the struggle under her composure, he felt no temptation to abate his stand by a jot. He had not yet formulated a reason for his resistance: he simply went on feeling, more and more strongly with every precious sign of her participation in his unhappiness, that he could neither owe his escape from it to such a transaction, nor suffer her, innocently, to owe hers.

The only mitigating effect of his determination was in an increase of helpless tenderness toward her; so that, when she exclaimed, in answer to his announcement that he meant to leave Paris the next night, 'Oh, give me a day or two longer!' he at once resigned himself to saying, 'If I can be of the least use, I'll give you a hundred.'

She answered sadly that all he could do would be to let her feel that he was there – just for a day or two, till she had readjusted herself to the idea of going on in the old way; and on this note of renunciation they parted.

But Durham, however pledged to the passive part, could not long sustain it without rebellion. To 'hang round' the shut door of his hopes seemed, after two long days, more than even his passion required of him; and on the third he dispatched a note of goodbye to his friend. He was going off for a few weeks, he explained – his mother and sisters wished to be taken to the Italian lakes: but he would return to Paris, and say his real farewell to her, before sailing for America in July.

He had not intended his note to act as an ultimatum: he had no wish to surprise Madame de Malrive into unconsidered surrender. When, almost immediately, his own messenger returned with a reply from her, he even felt a pang of disappointment, a momentary fear lest she should have stooped a little from the high place where his passion had preferred to leave her; but her first words turned his fear into rejoicing.

'Let me see you before you go: something extraordinary has happened,' she wrote.

What had happened, as he heard from her a few hours later – finding her in a tremor of frightened gladness, with her door boldly closed to all the world but himself – was nothing less extraordinary than a visit from Madame de Treymes, who had come, officially delegated by the family, to announce that Monsieur de Malrive had decided not to 55 oppose his wife's suit for divorce. Durham, at the news, was almost afraid to show himself too amazed; but his small signs of alarm and wonder were swallowed up in the flush of Madame de Malrive's incredulous joy.

'It's the long habit, you know, of not believing them – of looking for the truth always in what they *don't* say. It took me hours and hours to convince myself that there's no trick under it, that there can't be any,' she explained.

'Then you *are* convinced now?' escaped from Durham; but the shadow of his question lingered no more than the flit of a wing across her face.

'I am convinced because the facts are there to reassure me. Christiane tells me that Monsieur de Malrive has consulted his lawyers, and that they have advised him to free me. Maître Enguerrand has been instructed to see my lawyer whenever I wish it. They quite understand that I never should have taken the step in face of any opposition on their part – I am so thankful to you for making that perfectly clear to them! – and I suppose this is the return their pride makes to mine. For they *can* be proud collectively –' She broke off, and added, with happy hands outstretched: 'And I owe it all to you – Christiane said it was your talk with her that had convinced them.'

Durham, at this statement, had to repress a fresh sound of amazement; but with her hands in his, and, a moment after, her whole self drawn to him in the first yielding of
her lips, doubt perforce gave way to the lover's happy

conviction that such love was after all too strong for the powers of darkness.

It was only when they sat again in the blissful after-calm of their understanding, that he felt the pricking of an unappeased distrust.

'Did Madame de Treymes give you any reason for this change of front?' he risked asking, when he found the distrust was not otherwise to be quelled.

'Oh, yes: just what I've said. It was really her admiration of *you* – of your attitude – your delicacy. She said that at first she hadn't believed in it: they're always looking for a hidden motive. And when she found that yours was staring at her in the actual words you said: that you really respected my scruples, and would never, never try to coerce or entrap me – something in her – poor Christiane! – answered to it, she told me, and she wanted to prove to us that she was capable of understanding us too. If you knew her history you'd find it wonderful and pathetic that she can!'

Durham thought he knew enough of it to infer that Madame de Treymes had not been the object of many conscientious scruples on the part of the opposite sex; but this increased rather his sense of the strangeness than of the pathos of her action. Yet Madame de Malrive, whom he had once inwardly taxed with the morbid raising of obstacles, seemed to see none now; and he could only infer that her sister-in-law's actual words had carried more conviction than reached him in the repetition of them. The mere fact that he had so much to gain by leaving his friend's faith undisturbed was no doubt stirring his own suspicions to unnatural activity; and this sense gradually reasoned him back into acceptance of her view, as the most normal as well as the pleasantest he could take.

VIII

The uneasiness thus temporarily repressed slipped into the final disguise of hoping he should not again meet Madame de Treymes; and in this wish he was seconded by the decision, in which Madame de Malrive concurred, that it would be well for him to leave Paris while the preliminary negotiations were going on. He committed her interests to the best professional care, and his mother, resigning her dream of the lakes, remained to fortify Madame de Malrive by her mild, unimaginative view of the transaction, as an uncomfortable but commonplace necessity, like house-cleaning or dentistry. Mrs Durham would doubtless have preferred that her only son, even with his hair turning grey, should have chosen a Fanny Frisbee rather than a Fanny de Malrive; but it was a part of her acceptance of life on a general basis of innocence and kindliness, that she entered generously into his dream of rescue and renewal, and devoted herself without afterthought to keeping up Fanny's courage with so little to spare for herself.

The process, the lawyers declared, would not be a long one, since Monsieur de Malrive's acquiescence reduced it to a formality; and when, at the end of June, Durham 59 returned from Italy with Katy and Nannie, there seemed no reason why he should not stop in Paris long enough to learn what progress had been made.

But before he could learn this he was to hear, on entering Madame de Malrive's presence, news more immediate if less personal. He found her, in spite of her gladness in his return, so evidently preoccupied and distressed that his first thought was one of fear for their own future. But she read and dispelled this by saying, before he could put his question: 'Poor Christiane is here. She is very unhappy. You have seen in the papers –'

'I have seen no papers since we left Turin. What has happened?'

'The Prince d'Armillac has come to grief. There has been some terrible scandal about money, and he has been obliged to leave France to escape arrest.'

'And Madame de Treymes has left her husband?'

'Ah, no, poor creature: they don't leave their husbands – they can't. But de Treymes has gone down to their place in Brittany, and as my mother-in-law is with another daughter in Auvergne, Christiane came here for a few days. With me, you see, she need not pretend – she can cry her eyes out.'

'And that is what she is doing?

It was so unlike his conception of the way in which, under the most adverse circumstances, Madame de Treymes would be likely to occupy her time, that Durham was conscious of a note of scepticism in his query.

'Poor thing – if you saw her you would feel nothing but pity. She is suffering so horribly that I reproach myself for being happy under the same roof.'

Durham met this with a tender pressure of her hand; then he said, after a pause of reflection: 'I should like to see her.'

He hardly knew what prompted him to utter the wish, unless it were a sudden stir of compunction at the memory of his own dealings with Madame de Treymes. Had he not sacrificed the poor creature to a purely fantastic conception of conduct? She had said that she knew she was asking a trifle of him; and the fact that, materially, it would have been a trifle, had seemed at the moment only an added reason for steeling himself in his moral resistance to it. But now that he had gained his point – and through her own generosity, as it still appeared – the largeness of her attitude made his own seem cramped and petty. Since conduct, in the last resort, must be judged by its enlarging or diminishing effect on character, might it not be that the zealous weighing of the moral anise and cummin was less important than the unconsidered lavishing of the precious ointment? At any rate, he could enjoy no peace of mind under the burden of Madame de Treymes' magnanimity, and when he had assured himself that his own affairs were progressing favourably, he once more, at the risk of surprising his betrothed, brought up the possibility of seeing her relative.

Madame de Malrive evinced no surprise. 'It is natural, knowing what she has done for us, that you should want to show her your sympathy. The difficulty is that it is just the one thing you *can't* show her. You can thank her, of course, for ourselves, but even that at the moment –'

'Would seem brutal? Yes, I recognize that I should have to choose my words,' he admitted, guiltily conscious that his capability of dealing with Madame de Treymes extended far beyond her sister-in-law's conjecture.

Madame de Malrive still hesitated. 'I can tell her; and when you come back tomorrow –'

It had been decided that, in the interests of discretion – the interests, in other words, of the poor little future Marquis de Malrive – Durham was to remain but two days in Paris, withdrawing then with his family till the conclusion of the divorce proceedings permitted him to return in the acknowledged character of Madame de Malrive's future husband. Even on this occasion, he had not come to her alone; Nannie Durham, in the adjoining room, was chatting conspicuously with the little Marquis, whom she could with difficulty be restrained from teaching to call her 'Aunt Nannie'. Durham thought her voice had risen unduly once or twice during his visit, and when, on taking leave, he went to summon her from the inner room, he found the higher note of ecstasy had been evoked by the appearance of Madame de Treymes, and that the little boy, himself absorbed in a new toy of Durham's bringing, was being bent over by an actual as well as a potential aunt.

Madame de Treymes raised herself with a slight start at Durham's approach: she had her hat on, and had evidently paused a moment on her way out to speak with Nannie, without expecting to be surprised by her sister-in-law's other visitor. But her surprises never wore the awkward form of embarrassment, and she smiled beautifully on Durham as he took her extended hand.

The smile was made the more appealing by the way in which it lit up the ruin of her small dark face, which looked seared and hollowed as by a flame that might have spread over it from her fevered eyes. Durham, accustomed to the pale inward grief of the inexpressive races, was positively startled by the way in which she seemed to have been openly stretched on the pyre; he almost felt an indelicacy in the ravages so tragically confessed.

The sight caused an involuntary readjustment of his whole view of the situation, and made him, as far as his own share in it went, more than ever inclined to extremities of self-disgust. With him such sensations required, for his own relief, some immediate penitential escape, and as Madame de Treymes turned toward the door he addressed a glance of entreaty to his betrothed.

Madame de Malrive, whose intelligence could be counted on at such moments, responded by laying a detaining hand on her sister-in-law's arm.

'Dear Christiane, may I leave Mr Durham in your charge for two minutes? I have promised Nannie that she shall see the boy put to bed.'

Madame de Treymes made no audible response to this request, but when the door had closed on the other ladies she said, looking quietly at Durham: 'I don't think that, in this house, your time will hang so heavy that you need my help in supporting it.'

Durham met her glance frankly. 'It was not for that reason that Madame de Malrive asked you to remain with me.'

'Why, then? Surely not in the interest of preserving appearances, since she is safely upstairs with your sister?'

'No; but simply because I asked her to. I told her I wanted to speak to you.'

'How you arrange things! And what reason can you have for wanting to speak to me?'

He paused a moment. 'Can't you imagine? The desire to thank you for what you have done.'

She stirred restlessly, turning to adjust her hat before the glass above the mantelpiece.

'Oh, as for what I have done –'

'Don't speak as if you regretted it,' he interposed.

She turned back to him with a flash of laughter lighting up the haggardness of her face. 'Regret working for the happiness of two such excellent persons? Can't you fancy what a charming change it is for me to do something so innocent and beneficent?'

He moved across the room and went up to her, drawing down the hand which still flitted experimentally about her hat.

'Don't talk in that way, however much one of the persons of whom you speak may have deserved it.'

'One of the persons? Do you mean me?'

He released her hand, but continued to face her resolutely. 'I mean myself, as you know. You have been generous – extraordinarily generous.'

'Ah, but I was doing good in a good cause. You have made me see that there is a distinction.'

He flushed to the forehead. 'I am here to let you say whatever you choose to me.'

'Whatever I choose?' She made a slight gesture of deprecation. 'Has it never occurred to you that I may conceivably choose to say nothing?'

Durham paused, conscious of the increasing difficulty of the advance. She met him, parried him, at every turn: he had to take his baffled purpose back to another point of attack.

'Quite conceivably,' he said: 'so much so that I am aware I must make the most of this opportunity, because I am not likely to get another.'

'But what remains of your opportunity, if it isn't one to me?'

'It still remains, for me, an occasion to abase myself –'
He broke off, conscious of a grossness of allusion that
seemed, on a closer approach, the real obstacle to full
expression. But the moments were flying, and for his self-
esteem's sake he must find some way of making her share
the burden of his repentance.

'There is only one thinkable pretext for detaining you:
it is that I may still show my sense of what you have done
for me.'

Madame de Treymes, who had moved toward the door,
paused at this and faced him, resting her thin brown
hands on a slender sofa-back.

'How do you propose to show that sense?' she inquired.

Durham coloured still more deeply: he saw that she was
determined to save her pride by making what he had to
say of the utmost difficulty. Well! he would let his expia-
tion take that form, then – it was as if her slender hands
held out to him the fool's cap he was condemned to press
down on his own ears.

'By offering in return – in any form, and to the utmost
– any service you are forgiving enough to ask of me.'

She received this with a low sound of laughter that
scarcely rose to her lips. 'You are princely. But, my dear
sir, does it not occur to you that I may, meanwhile, have
taken my own way of repaying myself for any service I
have been fortunate enough to render you?'

Durham, at the question, or still more, perhaps, at the

tone in which it was put, felt, through his compunction, a vague faint chill of apprehension. Was she threatening him or only mocking him? Or was this barbed swiftness of retort only the wounded creature's way of defending the privacy of her own pain? He looked at her again, and read his answer in the last conjecture.

'I don't know how you can have repaid yourself for anything so disinterested – but I am sure, at least, that you have given me no chance of recognizing, ever so slightly, what you have done.'

She shook her head, with the flicker of a smile on her melancholy lips. 'Don't be too sure! You have given me a chance and I have taken it – taken it to the full. So fully,' she continued, keeping her eyes fixed on his, 'that if I were to accept any farther service you might choose to offer, I should simply be robbing you – robbing you shamelessly.' She paused, and added in an undefinable voice: 'I was entitled, wasn't I, to take something in return for the service I had the happiness of doing you?'

Durham could not tell whether the irony of her tone was self-directed or addressed to himself – perhaps it comprehended them both. At any rate, he chose to overlook his own share in it in replying earnestly: 'So much so, that I can't see how you can have left me nothing to add to what you say you have taken.'

'Ah, but you don't know what that is!' She continued to

smile, elusively, ambiguously. 'And what's more, you wouldn't believe me if I told you.'

'How do you know?' he rejoined.

'You didn't believe me once before; and this is so much more incredible.'

He took the taunt full in the face. 'I shall go away unhappy unless you tell me – but then perhaps I have deserved to,' he confessed.

She shook her head again, advancing toward the door with the evident intention of bringing their conference to a close; but on the threshold she paused to launch her reply.

'I can't send you away unhappy, since it is in the contemplation of your happiness that I have found my reward.'

IX

The next day Durham left with his family for England, with the intention of not returning till after the divorce should have been pronounced in September.

To say that he left with a quiet heart would be to overstate the case: the fact that he could not communicate to Madame de Malrive the substance of his talk with her sister-in-law still hung upon him uneasily. But of definite apprehensions the lapse of time gradually freed him, and Madame de Malrive's letters, addressed more frequently to his mother and sisters than to himself, reflected, in their reassuring serenity, the undisturbed course of events.

There was to Durham something peculiarly touching – as of an involuntary confession of almost unbearable loneliness – in the way she had regained, with her re-entry into the clear air of American associations, her own fresh trustfulness of view. Once she had accustomed herself to the surprise of finding her divorce unopposed, she had been, as it now seemed to Durham, in almost too great haste to renounce the habit of weighing motives and calculating chances. It was as though her coming liberation had already freed her from the garb of a mental slavery, as 69 though she could not too soon or too conspicuously cast off the ugly badge of suspicion. The fact that Durham's cleverness had achieved so easy a victory over forces apparently impregnable, merely raised her estimate of that cleverness to the point of letting her feel that she could rest in it without farther demur. He had even noticed in her, during his few hours in Paris, a tendency to reproach herself for her lack of charity, and a desire, almost as fervent as his own, to expiate it by exaggerated recognition of the disinterestedness of her opponents – if opponents they could still be called. This sudden change in her attitude was peculiarly moving to Durham. He knew she would hazard herself lightly enough wherever her heart called her; but that, with the precious freight of her child's future weighing her down, she should commit herself so blindly to his hand stirred in him the depths of tenderness. Indeed, had the actual course of events been less auspiciously regular, Madame de Malrive's confidence would have gone far toward unsettling his own; but with the process of law going on unimpeded, and the other side making no sign of open or covert resistance, the fresh air of good faith gradually swept through the inmost recesses of his distrust.

It was expected that the decision in the suit would be reached by mid-September; and it was arranged that Durham and his family should remain in England till a decent interval after the conclusion of the proceedings.

Early in the month, however, it became necessary for Durham to go to France to confer with a business associate who was in Paris for a few days, and on the point of sailing from Cherbourg. The most zealous observance of appearances could hardly forbid Durham's return for such a purpose; but it had been agreed between himself and Madame de Malrive – who had once more been left alone by Madame de Treymes' return to her family – that, so close to the fruition of their wishes, they would propitiate fate by a scrupulous adherence to usage, and communicate only, during his hasty visit, by a daily interchange of notes.

The ingenuity of Madame de Malrive's tenderness found, however, the day after his arrival, a means of tempering their privation. 'Christiane,' she wrote, 'is passing through Paris on her way from Trouville, and has promised to see you for me if you will call on her today. She thinks there is no why why you should not go to the Hôtel de Malrive, as you will find her there alone, the family having gone to Auvergne. She is really our friend and understands us.'

In obedience to this request – though perhaps inwardly regretting that it should have been made – Durham that afternoon presented himself at the proud old house beyond the Seine. More than ever, in the semi-abandonment of the *morte saison*, with reduced service, and shutters closed to the silence of the high-walled court, did it strike the 71

American as the incorruptible custodian of old prejudices and strange social survivals. The thought of what he must represent to the almost human consciousness which such old houses seem to possess, made him feel like a barbarian desecrating the silence of a temple of the earlier faith. Not that there was anything venerable in the attestations of the Hôtel de Malrive, except in so far as, to a sensitive imagination, every concrete embodiment of a past order of things testifies to real convictions once suffered for. Durham, at any rate, always alive in practical issues to the view of the other side, had enough sympathy left over to spend it sometimes, whimsically, on such perceptions of difference. Today, especially, the assurance of success – the sense of entering like a victorious beleaguerer receiving the keys of the stronghold – disposed him to a sentimental perception of what the other side might have to say for itself, in the language of old portraits, old relics, old usages dumbly outraged by his mere presence.

On the appearance of Madame de Treymes, however, such considerations gave way to the immediate act of wondering how she meant to carry off her share of the adventure. Durham had not forgotten the note on which their last conversation had closed: the lapse of time serving only to give more precision and perspective to the impression he had then received.

Madame de Treymes' first words implied a recognition
of what was in his thoughts.

'It is extraordinary, my receiving you here; but *que voulez-vous?* There was no other place, and I would do more than this for our dear Fanny.'

Durham bowed. 'It seems to me that you are also doing a great deal for me.'

'Perhaps you will see later that I have my reasons,' she returned, smiling. 'But before speaking for myself I must speak for Fanny.'

She signed to him to take a chair near the sofa-corner in which she had installed herself, and he listened in silence while she delivered Madame de Malrive's message, and her own report of the progress of affairs.

'You have put me still more deeply in your debt,' he said as she concluded; 'I wish you would make the expression of this feeling a large part of the message I send back to Madame de Malrive.'

She brushed this aside with one of her light gestures of deprecation. 'Oh, I told you I had my reasons. And since you are here – and the mere sight of you assures me that you are as well as Fanny charged me to find you – with all these preliminaries disposed of, I am going to relieve you, in a small measure, of the weight of your obligation.'

Durham raised his head quickly. 'By letting me do something in return?'

She made an assenting motion. 'By asking you to answer a question.'

'That seems very little to do.'

'Don't be so sure! It is never very little to your race.'
She leaned back, studying him through half-dropped lids.

'Well, try me,' he protested.

She did not immediately respond; and when she spoke, her first words were explanatory rather than interrogative.

'I want to begin by saying that I believe I once did you an injustice, to the extent of misunderstanding your motive for a certain action.'

Durham's uneasy flush confessed his recognition of her meaning. 'Ah, if we must go back to *that* –'

'You withdraw your assent to my request?'

'By no means; but nothing consolatory you can find to say on that point can really make any difference.'

'Will not the difference in my view of you perhaps make a difference in your own?'

She looked at him earnestly, without a trace of irony in her eyes or on her lips. 'It is really I who have an *amende* to make, as I now understand the situation. I once turned to you for help in a painful extremity, and I have only now learned to understand your reasons for refusing to help me.'

'Oh, my reasons –' groaned Durham.

'I have learned to understand them,' she persisted, 'by being so much, lately, with Fanny.'

'But I never told her!' he broke in.

'Exactly. That was what told *me*. I understood you through her, and through your dealings with her. There she was – the woman you adored and longed to save and you would not lift a finger to make her yours by means which would have seemed – I see it now – a desecration of your feeling for each other.' She paused, as if to find the exact words for meanings she had never before had occasion to formulate. 'It came to me first – a light on your attitude – when I found you had never breathed to her a word of our talk together. She had confidently commissioned you to find a way for her, as the medieval lady sent a prayer to her knight to deliver her from captivity, and you came back, confessing you had failed, but never justifying yourself by so much as a hint of the reason why. And when I had lived a little in Fanny's intimacy – at a moment when circumstances helped to bring us extraordinarily close – I understood why you had done this; why you had let her take what view she pleased of your failure, your passive acceptance of defeat, rather than let her suspect the alternative offered you. You couldn't, even with my permission, betray to any one a hint of my miserable secret, and you couldn't, for your life's happiness, pay the particular price that I asked.' She leaned toward him in the intense, almost childlike, effort at full expression. 'Oh, we are of different races, with a different point of honour; but I understand, I see, that you are good people – just simply, courageously *good*!'

She paused, and then said slowly: 'Have I understood you? Have I put my hand on your motive?'

Durham sat speechless, subdued by the rush of emotion which her words set free.

'That, you understand, is my question,' she concluded with a faint smile; and he answered hesitatingly: 'What can it matter, when the upshot is something I infinitely regret?'

'Having refused me? Don't!' She spoke with deep seriousness, bending her eyes full on his: 'Ah, I have suffered – suffered! But I have learned also – my life has been enlarged. You see how I have understood you both. And that is something I should have been incapable of a few months ago.'

Durham returned her look. 'I can't think that you can ever have been incapable of any generous interpretation.'

She uttered a slight exclamation, which resolved itself into a laugh of self-directed irony.

'If you knew into what language I have always translated life! But that,' she broke off, ' is not what you are here to learn.'

I think,' he returned gravely, 'that I am here to learn the measure of Christian charity.'

She threw him a new, odd look. 'Ah, no – but to show it!' she exclaimed.

'To show it? And to whom?'

She paused for a moment, and then rejoined, instead of answering: 'Do you remember that day I talked with you
76 at Fanny's? The day after you came back from Italy?'

He made a motion of assent, and she went on: 'You asked me then what return I expected for my service to you, as you called it; and I answered, the contemplation of your happiness. Well, do you know what that meant in my old language – the language I was still speaking then? It meant that I knew there was horrible misery in store for you, and that I was waiting to feast my eyes on it: that's all!'

She had flung out the words with one of her quick bursts of self-abandonment, like a fevered sufferer stripping the bandage from a wound. Durham received them with a face blanching to the pallor of her own.

'What misery do you mean?' he exclaimed.

She leaned forward, laying her hand on his with just such a gesture as she had used to enforce her appeal in Mrs Boykin's boudoir. The remembrance made him shrink slightly from her touch, and she drew back with a smile.

'Have you never asked yourself,' she inquired, 'why our family consented so readily to a divorce?'

'Yes, often,' he replied, all his unformed fears gathering in a dark throng about him. 'But Fanny was so reassured, so convinced that we owed it to your good offices –'

She broke into a laugh. 'My good offices! Will you never, you Americans, learn that we do not act individually in such cases? That we are all obedient to a common principle of authority?'

'Then it was not you –'

She made an impatient shrugging notion. 'Oh, you are too confiding – it is the other side of your beautiful good faith!'

'The side you have taken advantage of, it appears?'

'I – we – all of us. I especially!' she confessed.

X

There was another pause, during which Durham tried to steady himself against the shock of the impending revelation. It was an odd circumstance of the case that, though Madame de Treymes' avowal of duplicity was fresh in his ears, he did not for a moment believe that she would deceive him again. Whatever passed between them now would go to the root of the matter.

The first thing that passed was the long look they exchanged: searching on his part, tender, sad, undefinable on hers. As the result of it he said: 'Why, then, did you consent to the divorce?'

'To get the boy back,' she answered instantly; and while he sat stunned by the unexpectedness of the retort, she went on: 'Is it possible you never suspected? It has been our whole thought from the first. Everything was planned with that object.'

He drew a sharp breath of alarm. 'But the divorce – how could that give him back to you?'

'It was the only thing that could. We trembled lest the idea should occur to you. But we were reasonably safe, for there has only been one other case of the same kind before the courts.' She leaned back, the sight of his perplexity checking her quick rush of words. 'You didn't know,' she began again, 'that in that case, on the remarriage of the mother, the courts instantly restored the child to the father, though he had – well, given as much cause for divorce as my unfortunate brother?'

Durham gave an ironic laugh. 'Your French justice takes a grammar and dictionary to understand.'

She smiled. '*We* understand it – and it isn't necessary that you should.'

'So it would appear!' he exclaimed bitterly.

'Don't judge us too harshly – or not, at least, till you have taken the trouble to learn our point of view. You consider the individual – we think only of the family.'

'Why don't you take care to preserve it, then?'

'Ah, that's what we do; in spite of every aberration of the individual. And so, when we saw it was impossible that my brother and his wife should live together, we simply transferred our allegiance to the child – we constituted *him* the family.'

'A precious kindness you did him! If the result is to give him back to his father.'

'That, I admit, is to be deplored; but his father is only a fraction of the whole. What we really do is to give him back to his race, his religion, his true place in the order of things.'

'His mother never tried to deprive him of any of those inestimable advantages!'

Madame de Treymes unclasped her hands with a slight gesture of deprecation.

'Not consciously, perhaps; but silences and reserves can teach so much. His mother has another point of view –'

'Thank heaven!' Durham interjected.

'Thank heaven for *her* – yes – perhaps; but it would not have done for the boy.'

Durham squared his shoulders with the sudden resolve of a man breaking through a throng of ugly phantoms.

'You haven't yet convinced me that it won't have to do for him. At the time of Madame de Malrive's separation, the court made no difficulty about giving her the custody of her son; and you must pardon me for reminding you that the father's unfitness was the reason alleged.'

Madame de Treymes shrugged her shoulders. 'And my poor brother, you would add, has not changed; but the circumstances have, and that proves precisely what I have been trying to show you: that, in such cases, the general course of events is considered rather than the action of any one person.'

'Then why is Madame de Malrive's action to be considered?'

'Because it breaks up the unity of the family.'

'*Unity* –!' broke from Durham; and Madame de Treymes gently suffered his smile.

'Of the family tradition, I mean: it introduces new elements. You are a new element.'

'Thank heaven!' said Durham again.

She looked at him singularly. 'Yes – you may thank heaven. Why isn't it enough to satisfy Fanny?'

'Why isn't what enough?'

'Your being, as I say, a new element; taking her so completely into a better air. Why shouldn't she be content to begin a new life with you, without wanting to keep the boy too?'

Durham stared at her dumbly. 'I don't know what you mean,' he said at length.

'I mean that in her place –' she broke off, dropping her eyes. 'She may have another son – the son of the man she adores.'

Durham rose from his seat and took a quick turn through the room. She sat motionless, following his steps through her lowered lashes, which she raised again slowly as he stood before her.

'Your idea, then, is that I should tell her nothing?' he said.

'Tell her *now*? But, my poor friend, you would be ruined!'

'Exactly.' He paused. 'Then why have you told *me*?'

Under her dark skin he saw the faint colour stealing. 'We see things so differently – but can't you conceive that, after all that has passed, I felt it a kind of loyalty not to leave you in ignorance?'

'And you feel no such loyalty to her?'

'Ah, I leave her to you,' she murmured, looking down again.

Durham continued to stand before her, grappling slowly with his perplexity, which loomed larger and darker as it closed in on him.

'You don't leave her to me; you take her from me at a stroke! I suppose,' he added painfully, 'I ought to thank you for doing it before it's too late.'

She stared. 'I take her from you? I simply prevent your going to her unprepared. Knowing Fanny as I do, it seemed to me necessary that you should find a way in advance – a way of tiding over the first moment. That, of course, is what we had planned that you shouldn't have. We meant to let you marry, and then – Oh, there is no question about the result: we are certain of our case – our measures have been taken *de loin*.' She broke off, as if oppressed by his stricken silence. 'You will think me stupid, but my warning you of this is the only return I know how to make for your generosity. I could not bear to have you say afterward that I had deceived you twice.'

'Twice?' He looked at her perplexedly, and her colour rose.

'I deceived you once – that night at your cousin's, when I tried to get you to bribe me. Even then we meant to consent to the divorce – it was decided the first day that I saw you.' He was silent, and she added, with one of her

83

mocking gestures, 'You see from what a *milieu* you are taking her!'

Durham groaned. 'She will never give up her son!'

'How can she help it? After you are married there will be no choice.'

'No – but there is one now.'

'*Now*?' She sprang to her feet, clasping her hands in dismay. 'Haven't I made it clear to you? Haven't I shown you your course?' She paused, and then brought out with emphasis: 'I love Fanny, and I am ready to trust her happiness to you.'

'I shall have nothing to do with her happiness,' he repeated doggedly.

She stood close to him, with a look intently fixed on his face. 'Are you afraid?' she asked with one of her mocking flashes.

'Afraid?'

'Of not being able to make it up to her –?'

Their eyes met, and he returned her look steadily.

'No; if I had the chance, I believe I could.'

'I know you could!' she exclaimed.

'That's the worst of it,' he said with a cheerless laugh.

'The worst –?'

'Don't you see that I can't deceive her? Can't trick her into marrying me now?'

Madame de Treymes continued to hold his eyes for a
84 puzzled moment after he had spoken; then she broke out

despairingly: 'Is happiness never more to you, then, than this abstract standard of truth?'

Durham reflected. 'I don't know – it's an instinct. There doesn't seem to be any choice.'

'Then I am a miserable wretch for not holding my tongue!'

He shook his head sadly. 'That would not have helped me; and it would have been a thousand times worse for her.'

'Nothing can be as bad for her as losing you! Aren't you moved by seeing her need?'

'Horribly – are not *you*?' he said, lifting his eyes to hers suddenly.

She started under his look. 'You mean, why don't I help you? Why don't I use my influence? Ah, if you knew how I have tried!'

'And you are sure that nothing can be done?'

'Nothing, nothing: what arguments can I use? We abhor divorce – we go against our religion in consenting to it – and nothing short of recovering the boy could possibly justify us.'

Durham turned slowly away. 'Then there is nothing to be done,' he said, speaking more to himself than to her.

He felt her light touch on his arm. 'Wait! There is one thing more –' She stood close to him, with entreaty written on her small passionate face. 'There is one thing more,' 85 she repeated. 'And that is, to believe that I am deceiving you again.'

He stopped short with a bewildered stare. 'That you are deceiving me – about the boy?'

'Yes – yes; why shouldn't I? You're so credulous – the temptation is irresistible.'

'Ah, it would be too easy to find out –'

'Don't try, then! Go on as if nothing had happened. I have been lying to you,' she declared with vehemence.

'Do you give me your word of honour?' he rejoined.

'A liar's? I haven't any! Take the logic of the facts instead. What reason have you to believe any good of me? And what reason have I to do any to you? Why on earth should I betray my family for your benefit? Ah, don't let yourself be deceived to the end!' She sparkled up at him, her eyes suffused with mockery; but on the lashes he saw a tear.

He shook his head sadly. 'I should first have to find a reason for your deceiving me.'

'Why, I gave it to you long ago. I wanted to punish you – and now I've punished you enough.'

'Yes, you've punished me enough,' he conceded.

The tear gathered and fell down her thin cheek. 'It's you who are punishing me now. I tell you I'm false to the core. Look back and see what I've done to you!'

He stood silent, with his eyes fixed on the ground. Then he took one of her hands and raised it to his lips.

'You poor, good woman!' he said gravely.

Her hand trembled as she drew it away. 'You're going to her – straight from here?'

'Yes – straight from here.'

'To tell her everything – to renounce your hope?'

'That is what it amounts to, I suppose.'

She watched him cross the room and lay his hand on the door.

'Ah, you poor, good man!' she said with a sob.

FOR THE BEST IN PAPERBACKS, LOOK FOR THE

In every corner of the world, on every subject under the sun, Penguin represents quality and variety—the very best in publishing today.

For complete information about books available from Penguin—including Puffins, Penguin Classics, and Arkana—and how to order them, write to us at the appropriate address below. Please note that for copyright reasons the selection of books varies from country to country.

In the United States: Please write to *Consumer Sales, Penguin USA, P.O. Box 999, Dept. 17109, Bergenfield, New Jersey 07621-0120.* VISA and MasterCard holders call 1-800-253-6476 to order all Penguin titles.

In Canada: Please write to *Penguin Books Canada Ltd, 10 Alcorn Avenue, Suite 300, Toronto, Ontario M4V 3B2.*

In the United Kingdom: Please write to *Dept. JC, Penguin Books Ltd, FREEPOST, West Drayton, Middlesex UB7 OBR.*